Povee Ricson Series – Book 1

GETTING TO SEE THE MYSTERY

JULIE KATHLEEN

GETTING TO SEE THE MYSTERY
Povee Ricson Series – Book 1

ISBN: 978-0-578-80476-7 (paperback)
ISBN: 978-0-578-76548-8 (ePub)
Also available in Kindle format

Written and Illustrated by Julie Kathleen

Design & pre-press by Lighthouse24

Owner / Publisher:
JULIE KATHLEEN BROYLES,
legal registered business entity
Business Entity ID# 1066419500021
Minnesota Secretary of State
Filed February 1, 2019 – Active and In Good Standing

Website: www.truequantumorganics.com

Disclaimer

Julie Kathleen, the living woman, created this book,
and is name-holder of the legal, registered, business entity,
JULIE KATHLEEN BROYLES.

The owner, publisher, and copyrights holder of this book is
JULIE KATHLEEN BROYLES.
Business ID# 1066419500021
This business has full ownership rights to
everything created by Julie Kathleen.

Any similarities to places, events, names or situations, whether
real or fictional, is purely coincidence and unintended.

Introduction

These books are intended for the young child to enjoy. If the child is too young to read them, I suggest they be read to the child for their understanding about life and love. Children from the ages of eight to twelve are intended to be able to read these books, easily.

It might even be enjoyed by those who are older. I intend everyone who likes a book that is uplifting, to read these stories. May they spread love and kindness to all humanity.

Dedication

This book came from my love for children, specifically the young. I have so much I intend to teach them about life and love, family and friends, that it became clear to me: I should write it all down. After many months of planning, Povee Ricson was born. She is a young Guatemalan girl who lives with her family on their farm in her native country.

It's a fictional story that teaches those children who might not have family or homes, about what is possible in life. Children who slip through the system or have suffered from trauma of all sorts will enjoy these gentle books in this series. It shows them how to forgive and love others; even those who intend us harm.

I suppose these books will be overlooked by many, yet, I wish for the entire world to enjoy them and I make every attempt to create the interest for the reader to feel they are the main character. As Povee goes through her days, she grows up in the books. It becomes the story of a family making their living from the land. I teach about farm life to children who need to understand where food comes from, and if any one child realizes his or her self worth from my books, then I have accomplished my mission.

It's an effort of love that I write for the children. It's that same effort that drives me to continue to write for them. In this way, I hope to succeed in helping them find out about the opposite side of life; where hurt and pain is not an every day commonplace. I write for them, in deep love and gratitude.

Contents

Chapter 1
A Gift for Povee

SUMMER HAD ENDED for Povee Ricson just as the last bit of heat was cooling off in the mountains of her home. She and her family felt many hot days while they worked in the valley below. They could not go home to the farm yet, because down in the valley, there was still food to pick. They harvested quickly and together as a team, they completed the task; avoiding the scorching sun's rays. Midday was the worst.

If she could wish it, Povee wanted desperately to have a way to care for her family without struggling for food. This has always been what Povee has known; hard times. *Maybe other families go through this,* she thought to herself. *I must have the power to change this, someday.* Then the thought left her as she got back to picking fruit from a tree.

Later that day in the mountains, a rumbling could be heard and wind picked up from the West. There was nowhere to go from the pounding rain. So, the family headed home, loaded down and weary from the work.

Traveling by foot, they made slow time; and rough terrain made matters worse. Eventually, far into the evening, home lights could be seen. As she dropped into bed, exhausted, Povee dreamed once again of having plenty for her family.

When dawn came, Povee heard Grandpa calling for her to help him in the barn. She quickly dressed, ran downstairs and called out, "I'm coming!" Arriving at the barn doors, she had a glimpse of movement from one particular stall. This was her favorite stall in the whole barn! Today was the day, Missy's foal was born!

She made her way to the barn to find out what it was and if it survived being born. Povee discovered it was a girl pony that had been born in the night! She was so excited to see it that she forgot to ask Grandpa what he needed.

Making her way to the back of the barn, Grandpa motioned for her to pick up a small bundle to give to Missy. "This is extra nutrition for her to be able to feed her baby," Grandpa said. It was alfalfa: this is what Missy needed for her new little girl.

With the morning chores completed, they walked together to breakfast inside the house. The family was already eating and getting ready to go work the fields today. Povee and Grandpa ate quickly to spare time, so no one waited. With dishes done, they headed out down the mountain, to gather food for the winter again.

This walk is always so nice, Povee thought. *I love the smells of the woods and sometimes I see the animals peek out at me.* Having walked this path her entire life, she knew it by heart. It never looked the same, even though it was the same path. Nature formed the picture in different details when Povee walked it. Lost in thought, Povee got distracted with a butterfly, when all of a sudden, her family started running!

The hectic pace was a shock and Povee darted her eyes left and right to see what the danger was! In the distance, a group of gorillas were munching on bananas. They did not see her family. As the family ran, the gorillas looked up to see the family was too close. They became agitated. Then some started beating their chests in a display of power!

When a proper distance had been set, then the family slowed their pace down to stop and rest for a moment. *This doesn't always happen. But, when it does, it's quite frightening; because the gorillas are not friendly to people. I wonder if other families must deal with the same scares as my family?* This thought remained in Povee's mind throughout the day.

Chapter 2
Friendship with Singhon

LITTLE DAYLIGHT WAS LEFT when the family headed back home. Weary once more from picking their food to store over the winter, walking became labored and slow. Twilight lasted only moments, but Povee saw a shooting star and made a wish.

"I truly wish," she began, "to have more food and fewer struggles in the future." As Povee laid her tired body in the bed, she dreamed of the wish she made, and drifted off.

Morning came with the rooster's crow. Now Povee had different chores to do. This time of year is when the food is already picked, and now it was preparing the food, that began. Everyone had their own jobs and they worked together as one. This made it efficient so less time was used to complete the tasks. Days and weeks went by, and each day was the same, until the work was done.

Nobody liked how the work was so much, but nobody complained because they were all grateful to have food.

When Povee could, she managed to fit in a little time for play. The swimming hole, she and other children went to was the highlight of the year! It was a welcome period of rest and enjoyment.

And Povee made friends with some other children there, too. One in particular, a girl named Singhon, is such a good friend to Povee. She has a name that means "Lion Holder". It's a name that carries much honor in her country of India.

Povee had little experience with different parts of the world. Her home was in Guatemala. Mountains and the foothills were what she knew. When Singhon's family moved to Povee's native land, they brought with them some unusual customs that seemed different to Povee. Getting to know Singhon was fun to do because it was interesting to learn the culture of India.

Most of the time, there were no differences between them. Sometimes, the differences were due to traditions that Singhon's family would practice. This made Povee curious to know more about her friend. Clothing, food and spiritual practices were the areas of differences. Povee only knew that Singhon was her friend. Together, they enjoyed playing games and romping around.

Daylight was going fast on the days that Povee played. It felt like those days were shorter than the work days. Povee dreamed of having more play time to enjoy her childhood. In the mornings was always too much to do. "No one should have to work all the time," Povee decided. "This is not a good way to live." She made herself this promise; that she would find a way to help people have more fun in life.

Chapter 3
Riding Nagopi

SUNLIGHT DANCED in the window of Povee's bedroom, just as the rooster began crowing for the day. Getting up, she took food out to the barn to see Missy. Not long after, Grandpa came in to see her too. She was brushing Missy as Grandpa made his way to the stall, and Grandpa said, "Hi, my sweet little granddaughter! How are you feeling this morning? I love that you care for Missy. She is not young anymore and needs us to look after her now. It was a miracle that Missy had this foal. She must be very proud!"

Povee looked up at Grandpa to see his eye twinkling with delight at the new pony. They had not given her a name yet. Grandpa asked Povee what she would like to call this new one. After a minute, Povee decided to call her "Nagopi". It means 'hope'. This is what Povee has in her heart; hope for life and hope for the future. Grandpa said that it was a good name, and he nodded. Povee went over to pet the pony who nuzzled her hand in happiness.

I have many more moments like this; to feel that life is a treasure, Povee thought. *When horses nuzzle you, they must like you,* Povee decided; and she gave the pony a hug. Nagopi nodded her head and walked with Povee to the pasture for some sunshine. Missy followed close by to keep an eye on Nagopi. Many predators live in these woods. So, it was not safe for Nagopi without her Mom to protect her.

With summer harvesting over and food preparations done, Povee finally had time to enjoy her pony. As time passed, Nagopi grew bigger with each passing day to become tall enough for Povee to start thinking about riding her. This was done using horse training that was gentle to the pony. It was the tradition of her family to love their horses. How they trained ponies was kind and slow, so the horse understood what they wanted and agreed to it.

After months of practice, Nagopi learned that Povee wanted to ride her. Nagopi agreed to let Povee ride on her back. That started their friendship. Ever since, they have become close so that Nagopi senses when Povee wants to stop or go. Many happy days of riding Nagopi were in the future for Povee. She couldn't have been happier. Then something happened to change everything.

Chapter 4
The Dangerous Storm!

ON THE HORIZON, *a dark cloud rolled in. No one saw it coming until I yelled, "Get under cover, quick!" It was too late for many of my family. The weather had changed for the worst and I alone saw the trouble brewing in the sky.*

For the family who got caught, it was a nightmare out in it. The rest began running under shelters they could find. What happened next was so unbelievable; even I didn't think this was possible!

Lightning struck the barn, and all the animals ran everywhere while thunder cracked in the sky! Squinting to see where they all ran, I managed to spot out their paths. How to gather the animals was first in my mind. Next, I looked for family that might be in trouble. They had all found shelters to escape the danger. That was a relief to me.

Putting everyone inside got the most priority. Some were shivering from the cold rain and needed to warm up. Fireplaces were going and stoves had soup on, fully cooking.

That took care of everyone nicely, so we could talk about helping the animals get home. I heard my Grandpa telling someone that he needed their help in the morning. Finding the animals would take everybody looking for them in the woods.

I wanted to help Grandpa and I asked him if he would let me.

"No. You are not allowed to. You are too young to walk into the woods alone, and I need you here. Grandma has chores for you to help her in the house."

"No! I want to help!" I said firmly to Grandpa.

Surprised by my reaction, he gave in to the demand and said, "If you make sure to stay in sight, I will let you come with."

I hugged Grandpa for letting me go with and made my way up to bed for the night. I could hardly sleep with the excitement of the search for the animals. I had not been in the woods to find any animals before. This was going to be an adventure tomorrow. I tried to settle down for sleep and soon was dreaming of where they all could be.

Morning came, and so did my excitement! Rolling clouds dotted the sky like cotton candy. Any sign of the storm yesterday was gone, and I looked to glimpse if my pony was here.

Nagopi was gone! She had run like the rest of the animals. I was heartbroken to see her empty stall. If she was injured or hurt, I didn't know. So much emotion welled up in my throat that I choked on my breakfast.

Grandpa saw me upset, and he comforted me with words of assurance. "Maybe she's nearby," he said. "I think she will be found today. I will help you search." I needed to hear that and felt better soon enough.

To make matters worse, some of the family had head colds. So, they all could not come with. Now, Grandpa really needed my help! I felt proud that I was so valued to them all.

In half the time, we were ready and made our way out the door for the day. No one was sure what to expect. They had never had all the animals run off like this before.

I only knew that finding Nagopi was all I could think about. If she was lost for good, I would be so sad, that

I don't know if I could stand it. She was my best friend and I needed her so much that if I could not find her, I didn't know how I would be able to get up every day.

I love animals: that is true. The animals that we have, Grandpa cares about, too. When they are in trouble, it is most important to help them out.

I put animals first most of the time, since they depend on us completely for their needs. It feels good to take care of them and I enjoy helping Grandpa in the barn, too. Together, we have fun talking to them and making sure they are happy.

Walking in the woods seemed so silent and spooky; it made my neck feel tingly with shivers. I followed Grandpa to keep close, though he took bigger steps than me. Looking around, I saw no sign of our animals. It was as if they disappeared with no trace. I had to keep hope that we would find them.

Some of the family members were speaking about how the animals had no signs of being this way. Most thought we were looking in the wrong places for them. I then spoke up and said, "I remember a path they took! Follow me!"

We went on the path I saw yesterday, and in a little while, I spotted our first animal, grazing on grass. It was Nagopi! She looked up and saw me. Then galloped right at me to stop and nuzzle my shoulder.

Grandpa saw tears in my eyes and he hugged me as if to say, "It's ok now." I only laughed and wrapped my arms around Nagopi's neck. It was so much joy I felt, that I couldn't hear anything but Nagopi's breathing.

People began moving forward some more on the path and more animals showed up. Much relief was felt by everyone to see our animals, and we gathered them all into our group, to walk them back to home.

Chapter 5
Feeding Animals; Feeding Family

WHEN IT STARTED TO GET COLD in the mountains, we always put hay out for the animals. I was too little to carry those big bales of hay, yet I saw other children who could carry them, and I tried anyway. Mama said I should not, since I was not as big as the hay bales. That did not stop me from trying.

We are family who helps each other out. It is important that I can do my part for the family. We pride ourselves in being close and loving. If we do not choose to be loving, then we learn how hard life is without each other.

Since fall had set in, the animals could not get much grass. If they have no grass, they must get food in another way; and, this is why we give them hay. It has much of what they need to be healthy. I love fall so much! It is colorful and the air is crisp with hints of frost coming. What I would give to have fall be all year long!

Happy to be helping Grandpa in the barn, I made some piles of hay that the animals could eat. They all enjoyed this new treat and it showed as they eagerly chomped it up! Forgetting to eat my own breakfast, I ran down to a stream near our home that had many fish in it all year long. I loved watching the fish play in the water and they saw me looking at them. It reminded me of how we all are connected to life in many ways.

Mama called me to breakfast, so I left this pretty place to fill my own empty stomach with eggs from our chickens. They lay eggs for us every day. We have eggs from them all year long. Sometimes they lay too many, and we give those to the dogs to enjoy.

I have to try new foods, Mama says. So, I get healthy, too. When we harvest from the valley, it provides us many different types of fruits and vegetables. I love to see what they all taste like, so I know which my favorite is.

Nagopi likes apples as much as anything. She eats them out of my hand quickly! When I give her those, she gets impatient to have them. I am careful to not let her bite my fingers.

Having Nagopi be my friend, let's me tell her what I am thinking; so, I feel better if I am upset. She listens to me and nods her head. She loves me, too. I need her as much as she needs me. Together we are happy in our friendship.

After fixing more hay for the animals, Povee started walking back to her house, when a shadow caught her eye. It moved fast like it was trying to hide. She got worried that their animals were in danger. So, Povee started hollering out loud that a predator was near, to any family that could hear her. No one came, and she became scared that she might get hurt, too.

Chapter 6
A New Friend and Choosing School

MANY MOMENTS WENT BY *that I couldn't breathe from fear. I found my courage to seek out the shadow by putting a shovel in my hand; to use if I needed to protect myself. With shovel in hand, I tippy-toed forward and came upon that shadow.*

What I found was to be my next greatest friend in life! This was no predator. It was a kitten! How it got here and how it survived without its Mama was amazing to me. I looked for signs of its family but saw nothing, and decided to carry it home with me to show Mama.

At home, it was welcomed and named, "Welcome". I thought Mama was being funny. She said, "This little one needs to know he is always home here. So, he is ours now and he is safe." The kitten made purring sounds and snuggled onto my lap to sleep. I was so grateful to Mama for her open heart for another creature that was in need. We always find ways to feed our family and this was simply another one to feed.

If I started out thinking we had a difficult life, it was changing now. Each day was another mystery to solve that made me enjoy the journey. Our efforts were not more than we could bear.

I began to see how life is both, hard times and good times; not always easy, but rewarding in the end. If other families have life like this, then I think life is just this way.

Time made the kitten grow. Soon, he was huge! Welcome became fat! He loves food and comes running every time someone is in the kitchen. He loves to talk, too! It's noisy in our home now. I love him so much that I cannot get going in the morning without my snuggle time.

I don't know what I did without him! He is my favorite friend, besides Nagopi. Many mornings of joy come from Welcome. He follows me everywhere and I never walk alone without this huge, furry, orange kitty beside me.

Povee had to start school in the fall. That meant she could choose to go to the government school or she could choose to have school at home with Mama. With a decision like this, she looked for Grandpa to help her.

He always told her to follow her heart. That never failed to guide her right. If she did not follow her heart, she always got upset about something. This was no different.

The Guatemalan government made school for children to attend who could not have school otherwise. Povee felt lucky that her Mama knew how to teach. Not every Mama knew how, and not everyone had a Mama.

Povee wished this to be different, so all children could have choices. *Maybe someday I can change that too,* she thought. *If everyone had choices, then no one would feel left out.*

Chapter 7
Cold Weather

HAPPY WITH HER CHOICE, Povee wanted to stay home with Mama and the animals. It was a good idea since Grandpa needed her to help him in the barn every day. Welcome loved her being home, too!

Even though most of the day was taken up by chores, it seemed that learning was easy, now that she had to practice her education. Povee liked learning and she thought how it's fun to find out about people and the world.

In fall, when weather changes make cold mornings, Povee must bundle up to stay warm. Mountain temperatures are colder than valley temperatures and being higher up means colder and windy, too. In Povee's house, they have a stove that is heated by firewood. Stoves are the main way people in Povee's town heat their homes. She helps Grandpa chop wood every day for the stove.

They love the smell of fresh cut wood and food cooking on the stove. It feels good to have a home to be warm in. Povee knows there are those who need homes and she wants to help someday. She gives her heart out to everyone she meets. This is her way of loving them. She sees people who have much to offer, helping those in need and it makes her feel good. They are a community of caring souls that look out for each other.

Finding dinner ready, Povee headed downstairs after finishing up her homework. She needed the Math more. She thought that Language was easy, so she worked on Math. *This will help me in the future,* she thought to herself. Helping with dishes, Povee asked Mama, "How did you go to school?" It was not the answer Povee expected. "I went to school and had fun though it was not home with Grandma. I chose to go and had fun there." This made Povee feel good about her decision. Whether she went to school or stayed home, she was learning. It was alright.

The weather turned icy, so getting food to the barn made Povee cold. The animals all acted hungry every day. Povee saw they ate more and she realized it was because of the cold weather. They needed more food to stay warm.

As Grandpa helped Povee feed the animals the extra food, he was so bundled up that Povee thought, *I can only see his eyes!* They twinkled! That's the only way she knew it was him. Then, when they spread the hay, the sun's reflection sparkled on the icy ground. Povee wanted to get her skates out. It was time.

Chapter 8
Tracks in the Snow

WITH THE POND FROZEN OVER, the children in the area had made a playground of "Ice Capades"! Povee walked along the pond's edge, carrying her skates, seeing children skating on the ice. She found Singhon and came over to say "Hi."

Singhon smiled and waved at Povee to join her. Chatting and giggling, they enjoyed each other's company while a light dusting of snow fell on the group. One of the mothers had brought hot chocolate to share and she made cups of it for Povee and Singhon.

This was the traditional drink of Guatemala; cocoa. They always put cinnamon in it to spice it up, and Povee loved the dark, crumbly cocoa bars melted in hot milk. Singhon was not familiar with this drink. Her eyes opened wide as she tasted the sweet, syrupy liquid. "This is lovely!" Singhon exclaimed. "I must tell my parents about this! They will think it's delicious, too."

Time flew by quickly when they played. The sun began setting, so children were leaving for home. Povee hugged her friend, Singhon, and put her boots back on to make the trek back home, too. Kids were already gone when Povee started walking.

The snow had left an inch on the ground. She could see clearly because it made everything bright. She saw other tracks in the snow, too, that were not familiar to her. She found a set of tracks that were bigger than hers, and were not from people!

Povee grew alarmed that she might not be safe. She had to go through some wooded area on the way home. With over a mile yet to go, Povee was worried she had no place to hide from danger.

Matters got worse when she saw the tracks were freshly made. Povee had no training in protecting herself. She had a thought that if she made it home alive, she would ask Grandpa what to do next time.

Chapter 9
Wild Animals

HAVING SNOW ON THE GROUND helped Povee see far ahead all around her, and she squinted, trying to see further. As she made her way home in the snow, Povee had to lift her legs high, since it was deep in some areas. *I cannot imagine what made those tracks*, Povee thought.

"No!" Povee yelled as she realized what the danger was! Now, she knew what she had to fear!

Hungry wolves were roaming the area looking for animals to eat. Povee saw them before they saw her and she ran to climb up a tree, not knowing if they could catch her. They growled and ran towards her, gnashing their teeth! Povee was so frightened, she could barely hold onto the tree branch she was laying across. With wolves circling her, Povee only knew she could not come down from her perch.

In moments like this, Povee had many thoughts of how to help those in need. This time it was her needs first.

Having family meant there were people looking out for you. It was nice knowing someone was there to help in times like this.

Povee was in danger; real danger. She could not figure out what to do. She was very afraid of the wolves that made it clear they wanted to eat her.

With no way to help her own self, Povee started crying. This relieved some of the pressure of her emotions. That way she could think about more ideas to get home safely. Wolves never stop when they are hungry. She knew this from tales her family would tell. It was so late that Povee hoped someone would worry about her soon. This is exactly what happened next.

Mama asked Grandpa if he saw Povee recently. Grandpa told her he remembered Povee going to ice skating with other children at the pond. Mama let out a cry of fear, and then said, "Grandpa, she is not home yet. She is in danger!" With this sentence, he knew he had to get some family to help him go find Povee. Together, they took weapons to protect themselves and marched off into the dark of night.

Threading through the woods made many family members nervous. Animals lived there that were not safe to be around. This always was the main reason the family had to protect themselves.

Wild animals do not listen to people. They have their own ways of living and do not need people to tell them how to live. They can be aggressive and will fight if threatened. This is how nature intended wild animals to live.

The tame animals Povee's family has are totally dependent on the family to care for them. Those types of animals need help to survive. If no one feeds or cares for them, they can no longer live. This is what Povee knows about animals.

Now, Povee is learning about the dangers of wild animals.

Frightened, cold, and alone, Povee clings to her branch in desperation. In the distance, sounds of footsteps came near.

Chapter 10
The Love of Family

LASTING AS LONG AS SHE COULD, Povee hung on the tree. It was not possible to get down with those wolves underneath her. They continued to growl and jump up to try to pull her down. She had never been so afraid before, and she realized it was not a game. Povee wanted to wish it away. She had no understanding of wild animals that did not love people. This was a lesson she was learning that was a hard one.

Nearing the pond, Grandpa heard the wolves. He became frightened for Povee. Never did he think he would lose his precious granddaughter. Yet now, he was not so sure. In the moonlight, he saw moving shadows, so he readied his rifle for shooting. The family saw him and did the same to their rifles, too. It was a tense moment that felt like eternity.

In an instant, the wolves looked and turned, running straight for them! Aiming for the ground, Grandpa shot a bullet and the sound echoed through the woods like a cannon! This made the wolves stop and turn to run away.

The family, who had all been holding their breath, now could relax. The danger was gone, though not for long. Grandpa looked up to see Povee, clinging to her branch with tears on her face.

It made his heart hurt with sadness that Povee went through this experience without him. He wanted to explain to her all about wild animals before she ever encountered any. So, this shock she felt from what happened, he needed to heal for his little grand-daughter. Family gathered round the tree and lowered Povee into their arms. She held on tight, as the group trekked back in the snow toward home.

With Povee wrapped up in blankets and sipping hot tea, Mama stoked the fireplace to make it burn brighter for them. She sat down next to her Povee to speak softly. Grandpa went to get more wood as Mama continued comforting Povee. "I missed you and we worried about your safety. Grandpa and I realized you might be in danger and he took charge of finding you. He wanted to teach you about wild animals before this happened."

Mama reminded Povee about the gorillas she saw while on the path to the valley. "They were dangerous, too," she said. This lesson was not easy to learn, since Povee loves animals so much. Then Grandpa walked in, and sat next to Povee. Mama started washing dishes as the two of them talked more about it. Povee told Grandpa what happened and how she felt. This helped her heal from the shock.

Grandpa hugged her tightly and said, "My Sweet Little One, it's late and you need rest. I am here if you are scared in the night, since what you went through caused you fear. You are safe in the house. It's time for sleep. Goodnight Povee. I need your help in the barn, tomorrow." This made Povee feel better because it was their usual routine that she knew. She hugged Grandpa goodnight and went to bed.

Chapter 11
Trusting People

NO MATTER WHAT POVEE FELT the day before, she woke up feeling better already; because of the love she got from her family, the night of the scare. Since Grandpa was already in the barn, Povee ate fast and headed down to help him. First, Grandpa needed Povee to feed Missy. She was stomping in her stall, impatient for food. Next, he wanted her to help him get the cows to pasture for grazing. Last, he wanted her help to move all the sheep to a different pasture, because they ate all the grass from the one before.

Working with animals makes Povee feel good. She enjoys how they listen to her and do what she asks. If they do not understand what she asks, she tries a different way of telling them. Many tries are needed sometimes to get the information across to them. She has much patience for them because of her love for animals. Even after what she experienced yesterday, she still loves animals. The difference now, is that she is aware of the dangers of wild animals, too.

Soon, Grandpa had lunch for them both. He brought hot tamales from the house that Mama had just cooked. Povee smelled the wonderful flavors of the pork and her stomach grumbled with hunger. "I could eat them all!" she exclaimed.

Grandpa gave her several on a napkin, and she gobbled them up, quickly. "I love Mama's cooking," Povee said. "She is the best in the world!" Grandpa agreed with Povee and told her how Grandma used to make Tamales differently, because she came from Mexico where they put spices in it.

Povee asked Grandpa, "Where is Mexico from here?"

"It is about twenty days of walking from us, here, heading north."

Povee thought about that and wondered where it was. Grandpa saw her puzzled expression and decided to show her. "Here, Little One. Follow me." He took her hand and led her to a clearing in the meadow where trees had parted enough for them to see across the mountains. "This way is the way," Grandpa said, and Povee saw just how far it was.

Heading home, they took a different path, so Grandpa could show Povee more about where Mexico is. With the animals safely in the barn for the night, they walked a path up to a ridge above the farm. Grandpa let Povee look around a minute, and then said, "If you ever need to get to Mexico, this way is safest for you to travel." He explained to Povee about how people can be dangerous, too. Povee had already begun to wonder if that was true, because if animals can be, then, why not people?

As soon as she thought that, there became a sound behind them which didn't fit in with the forest. Grandpa turned quickly to reach for his rifle. Men on horses had gathered around them to stop them from leaving. Povee was frightened once more; not knowing these people and that now they could not get away. Grandpa smiled and asked how they were, in Spanish. The men did not smile; looking down on them with glares in their eyes.

Chapter 12
Grandpa's Wisdom

THE CIRCLE OF MEN came closer to them. Grandpa hesitated, and then brought up his rifle, aiming at the leader. They all stopped their horses to decide whether Grandpa would shoot them and the leader pulled back. "I came in this area to show my granddaughter the mountains. I am not trespassing on your property," said Grandpa. The men realized they know him, and apologized to Grandpa for scaring him and his little Povee.

With those words, Grandpa lowered his rifle and held out his hand to shake it with the men. They got off their horses and hugged and patted each other on the backs. All this excitement made Povee nervous, so she stayed close to Grandpa. He waved 'so long' to the group, and walked Povee home. Povee was quiet during the walk home; lost in thought about what just happened.

In the moonlight of evening, Grandpa gave Povee some seeds to munch on as they walked. She was hungry for dinner but they were not home yet, so he made sure she had something to snack on for now. "I am glad you told those men you were showing me the mountains," Povee told Grandpa. She wanted to be brave in his eyes so she said those words to make him think she has courage, too.

Grandpa smiled at Povee, giving her a hug as they walked back. She liked Grandpa's hugs because they made her feel better whenever she got upset. Kindness was important in their family and it all started with Grandpa.

He began this tradition many years ago when he had experiences that could have been made better by kindness. If Grandpa was not kind, he had learned how bad things could get. That is why now; Grandpa remains kind through all situations.

Povee thought that he was wise and she wanted to be like him someday. She made it her goal to follow his actions and words, so she could learn how to behave in the world. *I think that I am so much like Grandpa that I can have the same kind of family one day, too. I love Grandpa's ways*, Povee thought to herself.

Getting inside the house would prove difficult right now, as there was a problem brewing out in the yard.

Chapter 13
Stuck Plow

MAKING TROUBLE OUTSIDE, it was Farmer Ricoh. His plow had gotten stuck in the side of their house because his tractor had run off. Its engine was faulty, so it did not work properly. Grandpa looked over the situation and told Ricoh that together they could free the plow and repair the damage. That made Farmer Ricoh feel much better, since he worried that Grandpa would be angry.

When the damage was repaired, Grandpa asked Farmer Ricoh why he uses a tractor instead of horses or oxen. "I have wanted to switch to animals," Farmer Ricoh said. "But, my tractor kept working, so I used it."

Grandpa offered to take Ricoh to the next County Fair where animals are sold so that Ricoh could have his own animals to pull his farm equipment instead of a machine that breaks all the time. Farmer Ricoh was happy about that idea and thanked Grandpa for the offer.

They agreed to go next week and Povee asked Grandpa if she could go too. Grandpa thought about it a minute and decided it was ok, if Povee agreed to stay close next to him. Povee promised to stay right beside him the whole time. This would be a new adventure for Povee to experience. This was just what she always looked for; to see more animals!

Sleeping became impossible with new thoughts of her adventure running through her mind. *I wonder if they have any strange animals there*, Povee thought. *I hope to see many more creatures I have never seen before.* These thoughts and more were on her mind as she drifted off to sleep.

In the morning, she raced to get to the barn to tell Nagopi. The pony nuzzled her neck and nodded its head as if it understood. These were Povee's favorite moments; talking with Nagopi.

In fact, if anyone asked her, she would say that Nagopi was her best friend. Getting up on her pony, they took a ride out to the edge of their farm. Feeling the morning sunshine, warm against the chilly fall air; they enjoyed a morning walk. The sheep were out in one pasture, grazing on grass, when she and Nagopi cantered by. Leaves fell gently and breezes came through that whipped up the scarf on Povee's face. When she pulled it down to see again, she got a shock that sent shivers down her spine.

Chapter 14
The Sheep Dog Savior!

CREEPING FROM OUT OF THE WOODS, heading directly for them was a jaguar! Povee knew from her past experience, that all animals are not safe, so she began to fear for their lives! The sheep started running in a group, back toward the barn.

Nagopi reared up and Povee had to cling onto the saddle to keep from falling off. The jaguar let out a growl and charged at them, fully running now. Nagopi ran faster and got to the fence, jumping it easily to go stand next to the house.

Mama looked out her kitchen window to see the danger. Then from the corner of the barn, came a streak of lightning that was covered in fur and barking loudly; racing right for the jaguar! They both ran into each other, biting and clawing until the jaguar took off, back for the woods, limping.

Povee got to see the battle and squinted to make sure she knew what had stopped the jaguar. It was the dog they all loved, who guarded the sheep, Kunta! Povee knew their dog to be ferocious and protective, but she never saw him attack anything like he just did, to save the animals!

She got down from Nagopi and walked over to Kunta to check on him. This huge, beautiful dog all in white loped up to her for petting, wagging his tail. He seemed fine and was happy to see her. Povee felt so grateful that he was their dog. She asked Grandpa when she got back to the barn why he had that funny name.

"This dog is a gift from a friend who lives in Africa. The name *Kunta* means 'tree' and is an honored name from that country," said Grandpa. He loves his friend who gave him the dog, so Grandpa kept the name. "It is a fitting name, isn't it, Povee?" Grandpa asked. "You see how strong and true he is, like a tree? He cannot be budged." Povee agreed and thought about the names of people and things and what they all mean.

She named her pony Nagopi, because it means "hope". This is what Povee wanted; hope for life and everyone in it. She hugged Grandpa, knowing how much he must love his friend.

I am so happy this dog loves us, too. He protects our family. The sheep like being around him, so they all get along well. It's good to know the sheep are protected by this huge, beautiful dog they love. He sleeps with the sheep for their protection, as well. He enjoys being outside much of the time.

Whenever Povee wants to go into the barn, she knows he is there to protect her. It's good to have such a friend as Kunta to look out for her. He is the best dog in the whole world in Povee's mind. She loves him so much because he is always there for her and he is always happy to see her.

Then, in the next moment, a shadow was cast over them from above, blocking the sunlight. It hid the view so that Povee had to look up and she could see what it was.

Chapter 15
A Huge Shadow

NAGOPI STARTLED then jumped and kicked her hind legs in the air. Povee, who was standing next to Nagopi, let go the reins and stepped back to keep from falling down. She looked up to see what happened.

Spanning the entire sky over them were wings of a bird Povee had never seen. This bird's shadow was all around them for only a moment. It made Nagopi run into the barn in nervousness and Povee chased her pony. They all settled down when the giant bird flew away.

Kunta had chased after the bird, so it flew off; and he came into the barn, looking for Povee and Nagopi. Povee hugged her dog in gratitude, for he seemed to know what animals were not good to have nearby. Because the dog is so important to the farm, they feed him extra special food when they can. He does most of the guarding of the animals, day and night. Every farm has one dog they cherish, too. All families love their dogs.

When dinner was done, Povee and Grandpa sat by the fireplace, sipping hot cocoa. They had many chats at the fireplace in the evenings. This one was about that huge bird which dropped down and scared Povee. Grandpa told her to be watchful of those birds. They are Eagles.

Those birds eat small animals, but when they are hungry will also attack larger ones. Grandpa told her, "Always look around you, but you must remember to look up, too." Povee nodded and sipped more cocoa; while thinking about how wild animals are so very different from their farm animals.

In morning's sunlight, the snow came falling; soft as down, in waves of white. It was hard to open the barn door, to get food for the animals, today. Grandpa had to help Povee open the door. Ice had formed on the ground to block it. In came Welcome, to see what was going on.

"Well, look who's here," Grandpa said. Then he held his hand out for Welcome to come to him for petting. Povee brushed Nagopi, and put a blanket across her back so she would be warm. Did the same for Missy; then walked them out to the pasture.

The pasture was full with sheep. They searched for grass, but found few blades of it. So as hay was dropped in troughs for them, they all crowded to eat first. Povee thought they must be very hungry, so she set out more than usual hay for them.

It was a beautiful morning with sparkling snow on the ground. Everything looked so pure, with no tracks in the snow, yet. This made the farm look clean and new. *If no tracks are in the snow, then that means no wild animals are near*, Povee decided.

The day was so pretty that Povee thought it must be a Holiday to be so lovely! She was in her thoughts when she noticed movement in the distance. It looked like an animal, but she couldn't tell. Then Kunta came out of the barn to listen for sounds. He perked up his ears and looked in the direction of the movement. The next thing Povee saw was Kunta, running fast in the field toward the movement! He was not happy with what he saw, and she knew he was on to chasing something!

Chapter 16
Another Chase

IN THE DISTANCE, Kunta tackled an animal, and there was a scuffle before it ran off. Povee squinted to see what happened next. Grandpa had come out of the barn to stand near Povee and give her a hug. She loved it when Grandpa hugged her because he always made her feel secure and safe. Then Kunta came back to the barn to rest from what he chased out of the field. Grandpa said, "He is a wonderful dog, to love us this much. See how he keeps us all safe every day?"

I am thinking about what Grandpa said, and wondering, how does Kunta know when we need him? Is he is able to read our minds? I think he is doing something special; to know what we need. Maybe I will figure this out, in the future.

Now, it was time for heading back to help Mama in the kitchen. All the animals were happy outside, in the field we picked for them, today. Even Nagopi looked happy in the shiny snow-covered field. So, together, Grandpa and I made our way back to the house for some lunch.

Mama had fixed everyone jalapeno poppers with chicken soup. I loved those poppers filled with cheese and chicken soup warmed my belly. It took only minutes for the food to disappear because everyone was hungry. So, I cleaned the dishes with Mama. Then, we made lessons for me to practice, in Math. School was very fun to do, even though I was at home.

Povee had mastered her lesson today, so she got to go riding Nagopi. "I love riding you, Sweet Pony," Povee said. *It feels nice to be up on her back,* Povee thought. *I wonder if other children get to ride ponies, too. Maybe someday I can help other children have ponies to ride.* She dreamed about how she would do that. Then, Povee felt cold frost on her face and saw the Sun setting in the sky. She turned Nagopi around to head back to home.

Chapter 17
Holiday Gifts

WITH NAGOPI SAFELY IN THE BARN, Povee stepped outside to watch the stars. It's as if they were all lit brightly, just for her. Povee breathed deeply to smell the air. It had a scent of flowers in it, though those were hiding under the snow.

Crunching footsteps back to home; Povee had an idea to give Mama a gift. She gathered up the cleanest snow she could, and ran to the house. "Mama, I want to make you snow cones," she said out loud. Mama looked happy that Povee thought that idea up. Together they mixed fruit juices in the snow mixture and set them in the freezer to harden.

With the desserts made, Povee found Grandpa busy on his bench; putting leather belts together for his family. Grandpa enjoyed making these, so they had belts to wear. He also liked making suspenders, to hold up pants, and harnesses for the animals which go on their heads to help pull them along. Grandpa softened the leather with tallow which is from animals. The soft tallow makes it easy to wear, or it would be too hard to use.

Povee thought leather was difficult to work with. Her hands could not cut the leather very well. Grandpa told Povee that she would get bigger, someday; and she would be able to work with leather, too. She hoped she did, because this looked fun to do. Time flew by as the two of them made gifts for the holidays coming, soon. Grandpa said goodnight to Povee and they both had to stop working on this project, since it was getting late.

In the morning, Povee watched Grandpa finish up his breakfast to ask her if she would like to come to the Fair to see more animals.

"Yes! Oh yes, please!" said Povee.

"Well, bundle up, my granddaughter. It's too cold out to be getting sick," Grandpa replied.

This adventure was on Povee's mind, but she had forgotten about it. Now, Povee couldn't contain her excitement at the trip they were going on!

She bundled up as Grandpa instructed, and she saw that Grandpa was covered, head to toe, too. "My goodness!" Mama said. "I can't find either of you!"

Grandpa's eyes twinkled like usual, and they walked out to the barn to get Missy and Nagopi. "I'm driving this time, Povee," Grandpa told her as they hitched up the horses. "When you are older, you may drive this carriage for me." Povee snuggled under blankets they had across their laps, and Grandpa pulled the carriage top over them for protection.

The horses trotted along to Farmer Ricoh's and they greeted him at the gate. He was looking forward to going, so he waited for them outside. He was happy too, since he needed to buy horses for plowing. Povee went to the back seat so Farmer Ricoh could sit with Grandpa. She liked the back seat. It felt warmer. They trotted down the road to the fair; which was in another town, not far away. As they moved along, Povee noticed it was beginning to snow.

Chapter 18
The Fair!

ARRIVING AT THE FAIR, Grandpa secured the horses to the hitching post and helped Povee down from the carriage. He and Farmer Ricoh walked toward a tent in the middle of the fairgrounds with Povee close beside Grandpa as she promised earlier. Once inside, they found seats and listened to the announcer for the different animals to buy. These were all animals that Povee knew, except a few that she learned about.

The ones she discovered about were pigs, hogs, goats and ducks. She had never seen those before. So, Grandpa explained each one to her. It was very fun having this time in the animals' tent, because she loved learning new things. As they brought in the cows, Povee asked if they needed any. Grandpa said, "Maybe next time." Finally horses came out, and Farmer Ricoh looked them over. Grandpa said to choose larger horses that are strong.

Farmer Ricoh picked out two draft horses. Those were the biggest horses Povee had ever seen! Povee asked, "Why are they so big?"

Grandpa replied, "They are a different breed that grows much bigger than most horses do. They grow big, because where they originally come from, it was necessary for their survival."

Povee thought about it, and decided it must be difficult to live in the country those horses came from.

Farmer Ricoh hitched his draft horses in back of the carriage so they would follow it. Leaving the fair, they all agreed to stop at a food stand to get some treats. Gathering up snacks, Grandpa gave apples to all the horses, then handed Povee and Ricoh, some lemon tarts filled with cranberries to munch on.

"Delicious!" Farmer Ricoh said. "I haven't tasted these before."

Povee was too busy eating to speak. She loved the flavors of tart and sweet all mixed together.

While they were at the fair, snow had fallen more, and now it was very thick to drive through. Grandpa asked Farmer Ricoh if they could switch horses; since Ricoh's new horses were bigger and stronger to pull everyone along. Ricoh agreed and together they changed them out, putting the new draft horses in front. *Maybe they are tired*, Povee thought, as she patted her pony's head to reassure her.

The new horses began trotting and soon had the carriage moving swiftly through the deep snow. "It's amazing!" Farmer Ricoh said. "I love these new horses! They will work well on my farm."

Grandpa smiled; delighted that he could help his friend in need. They enjoyed the scenery all the way back home, while sunlight sparkled on the white landscape. Every hoof beat sounded solid, and the two new horses worked well together. Then another sound split the air. This one did not sound good.

Chapter 19
Mean Bullies

WITH THAT SOUND, came a clap of thunder and Grandpa looked up to see rocks sliding down the mountain right towards them! The horses in front reared up in fear and took off running. Grandpa held onto the reins tight to keep control of the carriage. They all held onto the sides to stay in their seats. Finally, the draft horses settled and slowed down. Just as quickly as it began, it was over. Povee let out her breath. She did not know she was holding it.

The two farmers got down from the carriage as Grandpa pulled to a stop. They patted all the horses talking softly to them.

"Those rocks did not just start falling by themselves," Ricoh said. "Someone set off a trigger up there."

Grandpa nodded in agreement as they both looked for signs of people on the mountain. From his view, Grandpa could see no one, even though he thought it was no accident. The farmers got back in the carriage, discussing what to do about that.

Povee was sad that people would try to hurt other people for no reason. She wondered what had made those people become like that. She knew that everyone learned from where they grew up. So, if these people had been in hard lives, then maybe they would want to hurt others to make themselves feel better. This was the only reason she knew that made people be mean bullies to others: if they had been bullied, as well. She thought someday she could change that.

The sun had already set, and in the darkness, Grandpa led their ponies into the barn. Povee went too, holding the reins of Nagopi as she tried to walk through the deep snow. Soon after, the horses were brushed, fed and settled in for the night. Grandpa helped Povee back towards the house.

"Grandpa," Povee asked. "What will we do about those mean people?"

Grandpa thought before he answered. When he did, his face was frowning.

"I cannot control those people. They have no conscience about hurting others. We can only look out for what they might do. That is the best way to help with this situation."

Povee knew Grandpa was upset about it, and she patted his hand when they were eating dinner. Grandpa smiled and hugged his Povee. She was the light in his life. Whoever those people were who intended harm to others, Grandpa knew someday, it would come back around on them. With that thought, he got back to enjoying his dinner of fried polenta with tomato, meat stew.

Chapter 20
Learning About the World

BECAUSE OF WHAT HAPPENED YESTERDAY, Povee was sad that Grandpa had to worry about people trying to hurt them now. She often had moments where she thought about how people in the world treated each other; whether they were kind like Grandpa, or mean like bullies would be. She has learned much by living with Grandpa. Mama tells her all about the world that she can. Now, Povee learns from the experiences she has with Grandpa, to find out what the world is like.

This day, she had a question on her mind and thought, *if people were mean to each other, who can they go to for help if they are in need?* She presented this to Grandpa to see what he said now.

He looked at his Povee who had such a question. He took time to think of how to explain to her how the world is. After some time had passed, he said this: "My Povee, you are so smart to ask me this question! I am proud to be the Grandpa to such a bright, young girl! No matter how the world is, if you remember to be kind, it will often change situations for the better."

This was new information to Povee! She thought the world changed you! Grandpa just told her that she can change the world by her kindness and thinking of it differently. Povee wondered if kindness truly changed what happens in the world. Grandpa told her that she can make it be a nicer world, simply by her kindness and forgiving others. With this lesson to continue, Grandpa reminded Povee that they were late to let Missy out of her stall.

After lunch, they went walking in the field with the animals. Together, they crunched in the snow, while crisp, cold air whistled around the trees. Many sheep were huddled together in a group to look for grass hiding under the snow. Missy and Nagopi had warm blankets on their backs. They romped in the pasture next to the sheep as Kunta came out of the barn to get his head patted and back scratched.

Grandpa hugged Povee and said, "This, right here, Povee; this is happiness."

She looked around her, seeing all the happy animals, the sparkly snow glistening white, and the smell of winter with sounds from the winter birds.

"I am so happy, Grandpa! I love this time of year!" Povee said.

Grandpa nodded in agreement. Then, he said, "I wish this time of year to be all year. This is when everyone remembers to be kind to each other."

It was only a moment for Povee to decide, Grandpa was right. She thought about everyone in her life that is kind. Whenever there was a need from the family, someone always helped out. It's the love that everyone has for each other that holds the family together. Grandpa made sure to help everyone feel loved in the family. He was the biggest helper of all.

After it got a little dark outside, Grandpa turned to Povee and asked her if she was ready to go in the house for dinner. Within a few moments, they were warm inside, having their meal together. Everyone was enjoying the conversation, when Povee looked out the window to see a large bird on a tree limb. It was turning its head completely around in a circle!

"I cannot believe it, Grandpa! That bird was spinning its head all the way around!" Povee gasped.

Grandpa chuckled to himself; for his little Povee was going to have another adventure, soon!

About the Author

JULIE KATHLEEN is a mother, grandmother and researcher of all things imaginative. When she isn't writing books, she is out gardening or inside playing with the cats.

www.ingramcontent.com/pod-product-compliance
Lightning Source LLC
Chambersburg PA
CBHW071930130726
47909CB00014B/2906